First North American edition published in 2013
by Boxer Books Limited.

First published in Great Britain in 2013
by Boxer Books Limited.
www.boxerbooks.com

Illustrations copyright © 2013 Emily Bolam
Endpaper illustrations copyright © 2010 Sebastien Braun
Text copyright © 2013 Boxer Books Limited

Library of Congress Cataloging-in-Publication Data available.

The illustrations were prepared using acrylic paint on 220g/m paper.
The text is set in Adobe Garamond Pro.

ISBN 978-1-907152-67-2

1 3 5 7 9 10 8 6 4 2

Printed in China

All of our papers are sourced from managed forests and renewable resources.

A STORY HOUSE BOOK

THE THREE LITTLE PIGS

ILLUSTRATED BY EMILY BOLAM

Boxer Books

Once upon a time there were three little pigs. They lived with their mother in a small, cozy house.

One day Mother Pig said to them, "You three are almost grown up.

It is time for you to go and find out about the world and build homes of your own."

So the three little pigs packed their bags, said goodbye to their mother, and set off to explore the world.

They hadn't gone far when they met a man who was carrying a bundle of straw.

"Please," said the first little pig, "may I have some of that straw? I would like to use it to build a house of my own."

"Of course," said the man, and he gave the first little pig a small bundle of straw.

The first little pig took the straw and began
to build himself a house.

His brother and sister went on their way.
After a while they saw a man who was carrying
a large bundle of sticks on his back.

"Excuse me," said the second little pig.
"Could I use some of those sticks to build
myself a house?"

"Certainly," said the man, and he gave the
second little pig a pile of sticks.

The second little pig took the sticks, and he got to work building himself a house. His sister said goodbye and continued on her journey.

She walked and walked until she saw a man with a big pile of bricks. "They look like just the thing for building a house," she thought, and she asked the man if he could spare a few.

"Yes, of course," replied the man, and he gave the third little pig some of his bricks.

Just about that time, the first little pig finished building his house of straw.

"What a fine house," he thought, feeling very pleased with himself. But just at that moment, who should come along but a big, bad wolf. The first little pig ran into his house and shut the door.

"Little pig,"
called the wolf
from outside,
"little pig,
let me come in."

"Not by the hairs
on my chinny
chin chin!"
replied the
first little pig.

"Then I'll **huff**,
and I'll **puff**,
and I'll blow your house down!"
cried the Big Bad Wolf.

Then the Big Bad Wolf huffed and puffed,
and the house of straw was blown to pieces.

"I'm going to eat you up!"

cried the wolf. But the first little pig ran away as fast as he could. He ran and ran until he reached his brother's house of sticks. The two little pigs hurried inside and slammed the door.

Soon the Big Bad Wolf reached the house of sticks.

"Little pig," he said, knocking on the door, "little pig, let me come in."

"Not by the hairs on my chinny chin chin!" replied the second little pig.

"Then I'll huff, and I'll puff,
and I'll blow your house down!"
cried the Big Bad Wolf.

The Big Bad Wolf huffed, and then he puffed, and the house of sticks was blown to pieces!

"I'm going to eat you BOTH for dinner!" cried the Big Bad Wolf.

But the little pigs were too fast for him.

They ran

and ran

until they reached their sister's house
of bricks.

Then all three little pigs dashed inside
and closed the door.

By now the Big Bad Wolf was feeling very hungry. He ran up to the house of bricks and cried, "Little pig, little pig, let me come in!" "Not by the hairs on my chinny chin chin!" replied the third little pig.

"Then I'll huff, and I'll puff, and I'll blow your house down!" cried the Big Bad Wolf.

The Big Bad Wolf huffed and puffed.

And then he puffed and huffed—
but nothing happened.

He took a great big breath and tried again, but
no matter how hard he blew, the house
of bricks did not fall down.

Still the Big Bad Wolf did not give up.
Quickly he clambered up to the roof of
the house of bricks and began to climb
down the chimney.

But just at that moment, the three little pigs took the lid off their dinner. When the Big Bad Wolf reached the bottom of the chimney, he landed in a pot of soup and burned his bottom!

As quick as a flash, the Big Bad Wolf jumped out of the pot and ran away as fast as he could.

The Big Bad Wolf never came back again, and the three little pigs lived happily ever after in their sturdy little house of bricks.